Aux trois petites filles: Jeanne, Cécile, et Mimi
C. C.

For my mother, the gardener,
who has a way with growing things
J. D.

Text copyright © 2010 by Cecil Castellucci
Illustrations copyright © 2010 by Julia Denos

First edition 2010

Library of Congress Cataloging-in-Publication Data

Castellucci, Cecil.
Grandma's gloves / Cecil Castellucci ; illustrated by Julia Denos. —1st ed.
p. cm.
Summary: When her grandmother, a devoted gardener, dies, a little girl
inherits her gardening gloves and feels closer to her memory.
ISBN 978-0-7636-3168-0
[1. Grandmothers — Fiction. 2. Death — Fiction. 3. Gardening — Fiction.]
I. Denos, Julia, ill. II. Title.
PZ7.C26865Gr 2010
[E] — dc22   2009015139

10 11 12 13 14 15 CCP 10 9 8 7 6 5 4 3 2 1

Printed in Shenzhen, Guangdong, China

This book was typeset in Diotima.
The illustrations were done in watercolor, pencil, and digital collage.

Candlewick Press
99 Dover Street
Somerville, Massachusetts 02144

visit us at www.candlewick.com

Grandma's
Gloves

Cecil Castellucci

illustrated by
Julia Denos

CANDLEWICK PRESS

Grandma has a way with flowers. She is always on her knees in the dirt, with her gloves on, talking to her roses, scolding the succulents, and laughing with the birds-of-paradise. Her whole house is filled with plants, and outside, her small yard is full of blossoms.

I run to her, and she folds me in her fleshy arms for a big kiss.

She smells like earth and coffee and hair spray and perfume. Those are my favorite smells.

Grandma takes her gloves off, and we go inside and wash our hands and put some hand cream on them and make me some jasmine tea. We eat the special secret cookies that she keeps in a fancy tin box or the homemade doughnuts that taste better than anything from a store and I tell her about my week and she teaches me about the garden.

Sometimes she repeats things. But I am very patient with her.

She always keeps the gloves near her, on the table or in her pocket, in case she suddenly needs to check on one of her plants or flowers.

Grandma always says, "You are my most special flower of all." And on hot days she waters me with the hose.

But one day Mama tells me that Grandma is in the hospital. We visit, and Grandma does not smell like herself. She smells like alcohol wipes, apple juice, and baby powder.

Mama thinks it is so sad that Grandma doesn't know who we are. Grandma thinks Mama is the hairdresser come to do her hair for a big party and that I am her childhood friend.

She speaks to me in French, because that's what
she spoke when she was little, before she grew up
and met Grandpa and came to this country.

"She's forgotten it all," Mama says sadly.

I tell Mama and the nurse that Grandma didn't
forget to water the plants in her room. They are big
and green, and the violets are blooming.

Mama gets the call from the hospital late in the night. I know it is bad news 'cause her shoulders slump and she cries as I watch secretly from the hallway. I see Dad put his arm around her and squeeze her shoulders just like he does to me when I am sad.

Everything dies one day. I know that. The old tree down in the park died. Billy's scraggly dog died. And now Grandma's died.

Mama and Aunt Jeanne have to pack up all of Grandma's things. People come over with food to comfort and help. There are old friends and family and even strangers.

All the people in the house talk and laugh and eat the cookies from the special tin. They tell stories about Grandma when she was young and alive.

No one seems to look twice at the plants with the yellow leaves, except for me. I slip Grandma's gloves on and pull away the yellow leaves like Grandma used to do, and then I water the plants and the flowers that everyone else has forgotten.

Everyone leaves after dark with some of Grandma's things to remember her by.

Mama says, "You'll get Grandma's locket for when you are older, and the porcelain ballerina is for your room."

"I guess so," I say, feeling sadder and smaller than I ever have before.

What I really want is Grandma and jasmine tea, and the hose on a hot summer day, and the homemade doughnuts that are better than anything store-bought.

I climb off Mama's lap and get Grandma's gloves
from the table.

"Mama," I ask, "can we can grow a garden of our own?"

"Yes," Mama says. "But I don't know much about gardening."

Then she smiles as she puts her hands out in front of her and lets me put Grandma's gloves on them.

"You can help me," I say, "to talk to the roses, scold the succulents, and laugh with the birds-of-paradise."

I will teach Mama everything I know.